BLOW THE CHINKS DOWN!

BY

ROBERT E. HOWARD

British Library Cataloguing-in-Publication Data
A catalogue record for this book is available from the
British Library

Robert E. Howard

Robert Ervin Howard was born in Peaster, Texas in 1906. During his youth, his family moved between a variety of Texan boomtowns, and Howard – a bookish and somewhat introverted child – was steeped in the violent myths and legends of the Old South. Although he loved reading and learning, Howard developed a distinctly Texan, hardboiled outlook on the world. He became a passionate fan of boxing, taking it up at an amateur level, and from the age of nine began to write adventure tales of semi-historical bloodshed. In 1919, when Howard was thirteen, his family moved to the Central Texas hamlet of Cross Plains, where he would stay for the rest of his life.

At fifteen Howard began to read the pulp magazines of the day, and to write more seriously. The December 1922 issue of his high school newspaper featured two of his stories, 'Golden Hope Christmas' and 'West is West'. In 1924 he sold his first piece – a short caveman tale titled 'Spear and Fang' – for $16 to the not-yet-famous *Weird Tales* magazine. He published with the magazine regularly over the next few years. 1929 was a breakout year for Howard, in that the 23-year-old writer began to sell to other magazines, such as *Ghost Stories* and *Argosy*, both of whom had previously sent him hundreds of rejection slips. In 1930, he began a correspondence with weird fiction master H. P. Lovecraft which ran up to his death six years later, and is regarded as one of the great correspondence cycles in all of fantasy literature.

It was partly due to Lovecraft's encouragement that Howard created his most famous character, Conan the Cimmerian. Conan – a barbarian-turned-King during the Hyborian Age, a mythical period of some 12,000 years ago – featured in seventeen *Weird Tales* stories between 1933 and 1936, and is now regarded as having spawned the 'sword and sorcery' genre, making Howard's influence on fantasy literature comparable to that of J. R. R. Tolkien's. The Conan stories have since been adapted many times, most famously in the series of films starring Arnold Schwarzenegger.

Howard was enjoying an all-time high in sales by the beginning of 1936, but he was also deeply upset by the ill health of his mother, who had fallen into a coma. On the morning of June 11, 1936, he asked an attending nurse whether she would ever recover, and the nurse replied negatively. Howard walked to his car, parked outside the family home in Cross Plains, and shot himself. He died eight hours later, aged just thirty.

A FAMILIAR STOCKY SHAPE, stood with a foot on the brass rail, as I entered the American Bar, in Hong-kong. I glared at the shape disapprovingly, recognizing it as Bill McGlory of the Dutchman. That is one ship I enthusiastically detest, this dislike being shared by all the bold lads aboard the Sea Girl, from the cap'n to the cook.

I shouldered up along the bar. Ignoring Bill, I called for a whisky straight.

"You know, John," said Bill, addressing hisself to the bartender, "you got no idee the rotten tubs which calls theirselves ships that's tied up to the wharfs right now. Now then, the Sea Girl for instance. An' there's a guy named Steve Costigan--"

"You know, John," I broke in, addressing myself to the bartender, "it's clean surprisin' what goes around on their hind laigs callin' theirselves sailor-men, these days. A baboon got outa the zoo at Brisbane and they just now spotted it on the wharfs here in Hong-kong."

"You don't say," said John the bar-keep. "Where'd it been?"

"To sea," I said. "It'd shipped as A.B. mariner on the Dutchman and was their best hand."

With which caustic repartee, I stalked out in gloating triumph, leaving Bill McGlory gasping and strangling as he tried to think of something to say in return. To celebrate my crushing victory over the enemy I swaggered into the La Belle Cabaret and soon seen a good looking girl setting alone at a table. She was toying with her cigaret and drink like she was bored, so I went over and set down.

"Evenin', Miss," I says, doffing my cap. "I'm just in from sea and cravin' to toss my money around. Do you dance?"

She eyed me amusedly from under her long, drooping lashes and said: "Yes, I do, on occasion. But I don't work here, sailor."

"Oh, excuse me, Miss," I said, getting up. "I sure beg your pardon."

"That's all right," she said. "Don't run away. Let's sit here and talk."

"That's fine," I said, setting back down again, when to my annoyance a sea-going figger bulked up to the table.

"Even', Miss," said Bill McGlory, fixing me with a accusing stare. "Is this walrus annoyin' you?"

"Listen here, you flat-headed mutt--" I begun with some heat, but the girl said: "Now, now, don't fight, boys. Sit down and let's all talk sociably. I like to meet people from the States in this heathen land. My name is Kit Worley and I work for Tung Yin, the big Chinese merchant."

"Private secretary or somethin'?" says Bill.

"Governess to his nieces," said she. "But don't let's talk about me. Tell me something about yourselves. You boys are sailors, aren't you?"

"I am," I replied meaningly. Bill glared at me.

"Do tell me about some of your voyages," said she hurriedly. "I just adore ships."

"Then you'd sure like the Dutchman, Miss Worley," beamed Bill. "I don't like to brag, but for trim lines, smooth rig, a fine figger and speed, they ain't a sailin' craft in the China trade can hold a candle to her. She's a dream. A child could steer her."

"Or anybody with a child's mind," I says. "And does-- when you're at the wheel."

"Listen here, you scum of the Seven Seas," said Bill turning brick color. "You layoff the Dutchman. I'd never have the nerve to insult a sweet ship like her if I sailed in a wormy, rotten-timbered, warped-decked, crank-ruddered, crooked-keeled, crazy-rigged tub like the Sea Girl."

"You'll eat them words with a sauce of your own blood," I howled.

"Boys!" said Miss Worley. "Now, boys."

"Miss Worley," I said, getting up and shedding my coat, "I'm a law-abidin' and peaceful man, gentle and generous to a fault. But they's times when patience becomes a vice and human kindness is a stumblin' block on the road of progress. This baboon in human form don't understand no kind of moral suasion but a bust on the jaw."

"Come out in the alley," squalled Bill, bounding up like a jumping-jack.

"Come on," I said. "Let's settle this here feud once and for all. Miss Worley," I said, "wait here for the victor. I won't be gone long."

Out in the alley, surrounded by a gang of curious coolies, we squared off without no more ado. We was well matched, about the same height and weighing about 190 pounds each. But as we approached each other with our fists up, a form stepped between. We stopped and glared in outraged surprise. It was a tall, slender Englishman with a kind of tired, half humorous expression.

"Come, come, my good men," he said. "We can't have this sort of thing, you know. Bad example to the natives and all that sort of thing. Can't have white men fighting in the alleys these days. Times too unsettled, you know. Must uphold the white man's standard."

"Well, by golly," I said. "I've had a hundred fights in Hong-kong and nobody yet never told me before I was settin' a bad example to nobody."

"Bad tactics, just the same," he said. "And quite too much unrest now. If the discontented Oriental sees white men bashing each other's bally jaws, the white race loses just that much prestige, you see."

"But what right you got buttin' into a private row?" I complained.

"Rights vested in me by the Chinese government, working with the British authorities, old topper," said the Englishman. "Brent is the name."

"Sir Peter Brent of the Secret Service, hey?" I grunted. "I've heard tell of you. But I dunno what you could do if we was to tell you to go chase yourself."

"I could summon the bally police and throw you in jail, old thing," he said apologetically. "But I don't want to do that."

"Say," I said, "You got any idee how many Chinee cops it'd take to lug Steve Costigan and Bill McGlory to the hoosegow?"

"A goodly number, I should judge," said he. "Still if you lads persist in this silly feud, I shall have to take the chance. I judge fifty would be about the right number."

"Aw, hell," snorted Bill, hitching up his britches. "Let's rock him to sleep and go on with the fray. He can't do nothin'."

But I balked. Something about the slim Britisher made me feel mad and ashamed too. He was so frail looking alongside us sluggers.

"Aw, let it slide for the time bein'," I muttered. "We'd have to lay him out first before he'd let us go on, and he's too thin to hit. We might bust him in half. Let it go, if he's so plumb set on it. We got the whole world to fight in."

"You're gettin' soft and sentimental," snorted Bill. And with that he swaggered off in high disgust.

I eyed him morosely.

"Now he'll probably think I was afraid to fight him," I said gloomily. "And it's all your fault."

"Sorry, old man," said Sir Peter. "I'd have liked to have seen the mill myself, by jove. But public duty comes first, you know. Come, forget about it and have a drink."

"I ain't a-goin' to drink with you," I said bitterly. "You done spoilt my fun and made me look like a coward."

And disregarding his efforts to conciliate me, I shoved past him and wandered gloomily down the alley. I didn't go back to the La Belle. I was ashamed to admit to Miss Worley that they wasn't no fight. But later on I got to thinking about it and wondering what Bill told her in case he went back to her. It would be just like him to tell her I run out on him and refused to fight, I thought, or that he flattened me without getting his hair ruffled. He wasn't above punching a wall or something and telling her he skinned them knuckles on my jaw.

So I decided to look Miss Worley up and explain the whole thing to her--also take her to a theater or something if she'd go. She was a very pretty girl, refined and educated--anybody could tell that--yet not too proud to talk with a ordinary sailorman. Them kind is few and far betweenst.

I asked a bar-keep where Tung Yin lived and he told me. "But," he added, "you better keep away from Tung Yin. He's a shady customer and he don't like whites."

"You're nuts," I said. "Any man which Miss Kit Worley works for is bound to be okay."

"Be that as it may," said the bar-keep. "The cops think that Tung Yin was some way mixed up in the big diamond theft."

"What big diamond theft?" I said.

"Gee whiz," he said. "Didn't you hear about the big diamond theft last month?"

"Last month I was in Australia," I said impatiently.

"Well," he said, "somebody stole the Royal Crystal-- that's what they called the diamond account of a emperor of China once usin' it to tell fortunes, like the gypsies use a crystal ball, y'know. Somebody stole it right outa the government museum. Doped the guards, hooked the stone and got clean away. Slickest thing I ever heard of in my life. That diamond's worth a fortune. And some think that Tung Yin had a hand in it. Regular international ruckus. They got Sir Peter Brent, the big English detective, workin' on the case now."

"Well," I said, "I ain't interested. Only I know Tung Yin never stole it, because Miss Worley wouldn't work for nobody but a gent."

SO I WENT TO TUNG YIN'S place. It was a whopping big house, kinda like a palace, off some distance from the main part of the city. I went in a 'ricksha and got there just before sundown. The big house was set out by itself amongst groves of orange trees and cherry trees and the like, and I seen a airplane out in a open space that was fixed up like a landing field. I remembered that I'd heard tell that Tung Yin had a young Australian aviator named Clanry in his employ. I figgered likely that was his plane.

I started for the house and then got cold feet. I hadn't never been in a rich Chinee's dump before and I didn't know how to go about it. I didn't know whether you was supposed to go up and knock on the door and ask for Miss Kit Worley, or what. So I decided I'd cruise around a little and maybe I'd see her walking in the garden. I come up to the garden, which had a high wall around it, and I climbed up on the wall and looked over. They was lots of flowers and cherry trees and a fountain with a bronze dragon, and over near the back of the big house they was another low wall, kind of separating the house from the garden. And I seen a feminine figger pass through a small gate in this wall.

Taking a chance it was Miss Worley, I dropped into the garden, hastened forward amongst the cherry trees and flowers, and blundered through the gate into a kind of small court. Nobody was there, but I seen a door just closing in the house so I went right on through and come into a room furnished in the usual Chinese style, with tapestries and screens and silk cushions and them funny Chinese tea tables and things. A chorus of startled feminine squeals brung me up standing and I gawped about in confusion. Miss Worley wasn't nowhere in sight. All I seen was three or four Chinese girls which looked at me like I was a sea serpent.

"What you do here?" asked one of them.

"I'm lookin' for the governess," I said, thinking that maybe these was Tung Yin's nieces. Though, by golly, I never seen no girls which had less of the schoolgirl look about 'em.

"Governor?" she said. "You crazee? Governor him live along Nanking."

"Naw, naw," I said. "Gover-ness, see? The young lady which governesses the big boy's nieces--Tung Yin's nieces."

"You crazee," she said decisively. "Tung Yin him got no fool nieces."

"Say, listen," I said. "We ain't gettin' nowhere. I can't speak Chinee and you evidently can't understand English. I'm lookin' for Miss Kit Worley, see?"

"Ooooh!" she understood all right and looked at me with her slant eyes widened. They all got together and whispered while I got nervouser and nervouser. I didn't like the look of things, somehow. Purty soon she said: "Mees Worley she not live along here no more. She gone."

11

"Well," I said vaguely, "I reckon I better be goin'." I started for the door, but she grabbed me. "Wait," she said. "You lose your head, suppose you go that way."

"Huh?" I grunted, slightly shocked and most unpleasantly surprised. "What? I ain't done nothin'."

She made a warning gesture and turning to one of the other girls said: "Go fetch Yuen Tang."

The other girl looked surprised: "Yuen Tang?" she said kind of dumb-like, like she didn't understand. The first girl snapped something at her in Chinee and give her a disgusted push through the door. Then she turned to me.

"Tung Yin no like white devils snooping around," she said with a shake of her head. "Suppose he find you here, he cut your head off--snick," she said dramatically, jerking her finger acrost her throat.

I will admit cold sweat bust out on me.

"Great cats," I said plaintively. "I thought this Tung Yin was a respectable merchant. I ain't never heard he was a mysterious mandarin or a brigand or somethin'. Stand away from that door, sister. I'm makin' tracks."

Again she shook her head and laying a finger to her lips cautiously, she beckoned me to look through the door by which I'd entered. The gate opening into the garden from the courtyard was partly open.

What I seen made my hair stand up. It was nearly dark. The garden looked shadowy and mysterious, but it was still light enough for me to make out the figgers of five big coolies sneaking along with long curved knives in their hands.

"They look for you," whispered the girl. "Tung Yin fear spies. They know somebody climb the wall. Wait, we hide you."

THEY GRABBED ME AND pushed me into a kind of closet and shut the door, leaving me in total darkness. How long I stood there sweating with fear and nervousness, I never knowed. I couldn't hear much in there and what I did hear was muffled, but it seemed like they was a lot of whispering and muttering going on through the house. Once I heard a kind of galloping like a lot of men running, then they was some howls and what sounded like a voice swearing in English.

Then at last the door opened. A Chinaman in the garb of a servant looked in and I was about to bust him one, when I seen the Chinese girl looking over his shoulder.

"Come out cautiously," he said, in his hissing English. "I am your friend and would aid you to escape, but if you do not follow my directions exactly, you will not live to see the sunrise. Tung Yin will butcher you."

"Holy cats," I said vaguely. "What's he got it in for me for? I ain't done nothin'."

"He mistrusts all men," said the Chinaman. "I am Yuen Tang and I hate his evil ways, though circumstances have forced me to do his bidding. Come."

That was a nice mess for a honest seaman to get into, hey? I followed Yuen Tang and the girl, sweating profusely, and they led me through long, deserted corridors and finally stopped before a heavy barred door.

"Through this door lies freedom," hissed Yuen Tang. "To escape from the house of Tung Yin you must cross the chamber which lies beyond this portal. Once through, you will come to an outer door and liberty. Here." He shoved a small but wicked looking pistol into my hand.

"What's that for?" I asked nervously, recoiling. "I don't like them things."

"You may have to shoot your way through," he whispered. "No man knows the guile of Tung Yin. In the darkness of the chamber he may come upon you with murder in his hand."

"Oh gosh," I gasped wildly. "Ain't they no other way out?"

"None other," said Yuen Tang. "You must take your chance."

I felt like my legs was plumb turning to taller. And then I got mad. Here was me, a peaceful, law-abiding sailorman, being hounded and threatened by a blame yellow-belly I hadn't never even seen.

"Gimme that gat," I growled. "I ain't never used nothin' but my fists in a fray, but I ain't goin' to let no Chinee carve me up if I can help it."

"Good," purred Yuen Tang. "Take the gun and go swiftly. If you hear a sound in the darkness, shoot quick and straight."

So, shoving the gun into my sweaty fingers, him and the girl opened the door, pushed me through and shut the door behind me. I turned quick and pushed at it. They'd barred it on the other side and I could of swore I heard a sort of low snicker.

I strained my eyes trying to see something. It was as dark as anything. I couldn't see nothing nor hear nothing. I started groping my way forward, then stopped short. Somewhere I heard a door open stealthily. I started sweating. I couldn't see nothing at all, but I heard the door close again, a bolt slid softly into place and I had the uncanny sensation that they was somebody in that dark room with me.

CUSSING FIERCELY TO myself because my hand shook so, I poked the gun out ahead of me and waited. A stealthy sound came to me from the other side of the chamber and I pulled the trigger wildly. A flash of fire stabbed back at me and I heard the lead sing past my ear as I ducked wildly. I was firing blindly, as fast as I could jerk the trigger, figgering on kind of swamping him with the amount of lead I was throwing his way. And he was shooting back just as fast. I seen the flash spitting in a continual stream of fire and the air was full of lead, from the sound. I heard the bullets sing past my ears so close they nearly combed my hair, and spat on the wall behind me. My hair stood straight up, but I kept on jerking the trigger till the gun was empty and no answering shots came.

Aha, I thought, straightening up. I've got him. And at that instant, to my rage and amazement, there sounded a metallic click from the darkness. It was incredible I should miss all them shots, even in the dark. But it must be so, I thought wrathfully. He wasn't laying on the floor full of lead; his gun was empty too. I knowed that sound was the hammer snapping on a empty shell.

And I got real mad. I seen red. I throwed away the gun and, cussing silently, got on my all-fours and begun to crawl stealthily but rapidly acrost the floor. If he had a knife, this mode of attack would give me some advantage.

That was a blame big chamber. I judge I'd traversed maybe half the distance across it when my head come into violent contact with what I instinctively realized was a human skull. My opponent had got the same idee I had. Instantly we throwed ourselves ferociously on each other and there begun a most desperate battle in the dark. My unseen foe didn't seem to have no knife, but he was a bearcat in action. I was doing my best, slugging, kicking, rassling and ever and anon sinking my fangs into his hide, but I never see the Chinaman that could fight like this 'un fought. I never seen one which could use his fists, but this 'un could.

I heard 'em swish past my head in the dark and purty soon I stopped one of them fists with my nose. Whilst I was trying to shake the blood and stars outa my eyes, my raging opponent clamped his teeth in my ear and set back. With a maddened roar, I hooked him in the belly with such heartiness that he let go with a gasp and curled up like a angle-worm. I then climbed atop of him and set to work punching him into a pulp, but he come to hisself under my very fists, as it were, pitched me off and got a scissors hold that nearly caved my ribs in.

Gasping for breath, I groped around and having found one of his feet, got a toe-hold and started twisting it off. He give a ear-piercing and bloodthirsty yell and jarred me loose with a terrific kick in the neck.

We arose and fanned the air with wild swings, trying to find each other in the dark. After nearly throwing our arms out of place missing haymakers, we abandoned this futile and aimless mode of combat and having stumbled into each other, we got each other by the neck with our lefts and hammered away with our rights.

A minute or so of this satisfied my antagonist, who, after a vain attempt to find my right and tie it up, throwed hisself blindly and bodily at me. We went to the floor together. I got a strangle hold on him and soon had him gurgling spasmodically. A chance swat on the jaw jarred me loose, but I come back with a blind swing that by pure chance crunched solidly into his mouth. Again we locked horns and tumbled about on the floor.

"DERN YOUR YELLER hide," said the Chinaman between gasps. "You're the toughest Chinee I ever fit in my life, but I'll get you yet!"

"Bill McGlory," I said in disgust. "What you doin' here?"

"By golly," said he. "If I didn't know you was Tung Yin, I'd swear you was Steve Costigan."

"I am Steve Costigan, you numb-skull," I said impatiently, hauling him to his feet.

"Well, gee whiz," he said. "Them girls told me I might have to shoot Tung Yin to make my getaway, but they didn't say nothin' about you. Where is the big shot?"

"How should I know?" I snapped. "Yuen Tang and a girl told me Tung Yin was goin' to chop my head off. And they gimme a gun and pushed me in here. What you doin' anyway?"

"I come here to see Miss Worley," he said. "She'd done left when I went back to the La Belle. I looked around the streets for her, then I decided I'd come out to Tung Yin's and see her."

"And who told you you could come callin' on her?" I snarled.

"Well," he said smugly, "anybody could see that girl had fell for me. As far as that goes, who told you to come chasin' after her?"

"That's entirely different," I growled. "Go ahead with your story."

"Well," he said, "I come and knocked on the door and a Chinaman opened it and I asked for Miss Worley and he slammed the door in my face. That made me mad, so I prowled around and found a gate unlocked in the garden wall and come in, hopin' to find her in the garden. But a gang of tough lookin' coolies spotted me and though I tried to explain my peaceful intentions, they got hard and started wavin' knives around.

"Well, Steve, you know me. I'm a peaceful man but I ain't goin' be tromped on. I got rights, by golly. I hauled off and knocked the biggest one as cold as a wedge. Then I lit out and they run me clean through the garden. Every time I made for the wall, they headed me off, so I run through the courtyard into the house and smack into Tung Yin hisself. I knowed him by sight, you see. He had a golden pipe-case which he was lookin' at like he thought it was a million dollars or somethin'. When he seen me, he quick stuck it in his shirt and give a yelp like he was stabbed.

"I tried to explain, but he started yelling to the coolies in Chinese and they bust in after me. I run through a door ahead of 'em and slammed it in their faces and bolted it, and whilst I was holding it on one side and they was tryin' to kick it down on the other side, up come a Chinagirl which told me in broken English that she'd help me, and she hid me in a closet. Purty soon her and a coolie come and said that Tung Yin was huntin' me in another part of the house, and that they'd help me escape. So they took me to a door and gimme a gun and said if I could get through the room I'd be safe. Then they shoved me in here and bolted the door behind me. The next thing I knowed, bullets was singin' past my ears like a swarm of bees. You sure are a rotten shot, Steve."

"You ain't so blamed hot yourself," I sniffed. "Anyway, it looks to me like we been took plenty, and you sure are lucky to be alive. For some reason or other Tung Yin wanted to get rid of us and he seen a good way to do it without no risk to his own hide, by gyppin' us into bumpin' each other off. Wait, though--looks to me like that mutt Yuen Tang engineered this deal. Maybe Tung Yin didn't know nothin' about it."

"Well, anyway," said Bill, "they's somethin' crooked goin' on here that these Chinese don't want known. They think we're government spies, I betcha."

"Well, let's get outa here," I said.

"I bet they think we're both dead," said Bill. "They told me these walls was sound-proof. I bet they use this for a regular murder room. I been hearin' a lot of dark tales about

Tung Yin. I'm surprised a nice girl like Miss Worley would work for him."

"Aw," I said, "we musta misunderstood her. She don't work here. The Chinagirls told me so. He ain't got no nieces. It musta been somebody else."

"Well let's get out and argy later," Bill said. "Come on, let's feel around and find a door."

"Well," I said, "what good'll that do? The doors is bolted, ain't they?"

"Well, my gosh," he said, "can't we bust 'em down? Gee whiz, you'd stop to argy if they was goin' to shoot you."

We felt around and located the walls and we hadn't been groping long before I found what I knowed was bound to be a door. I told Bill and he come feeling his way along the wall. Then I heard something else.

"Easy, Bill," I whispered. "Somebody's unboltin' this door from the other side."

STANDING THERE SILENTLY, we plainly heard the sound of bolts being drawn. Then the door began opening and a crack of light showed. We flattened ourselves on either side of the door and waited, nerves tense and jumping.

Right then my white bulldog, Mike, could 'a' been able to help, if he hadn't been laid up with distemper.

The door opened. A Chinaman stuck his head in, grinning nastily. He had a electric torch in his hand and he was flashing it around over the floor--to locate the corpses, I reckon.

Before he had time to realize they wasn't no corpses, I grabbed him by the neck and jerked him headlong into the room. Bill connected a heavy right swing with his jaw. The Chinee stiffened, out cold. I let him fall careless-like to the floor. He'd dropped the light when Bill socked him. It went out when it hit the floor, but Bill groped around, and found it and flashed it on.

"Let's go," said Bill, so we went into the dark corridor outside and shut the door and bolted it. Bill flashed his light around, for it was dark in the corridor. We went along it and come through a door. Lights was on in that chamber, and in them adjoining it, but everything was still and deserted. We stole very warily through the rooms but we seen nobody, neither coolies, servants nor girls.

The house was kind of disheveled and tumbled about. Some of the hangings and things was gone. Things was kind of jerked around like the people had left all of a sudden, taking part of their belongings with 'em.

"By golly," said Bill. "This here's uncanny. They've moved out and left it with us."

I was opening a door and started to answer, then stopped short. In the room beyond, almost within arm's length, as I seen through the half open door, was Yuen Tang. But he wasn't dressed in servant's clothes no more. He looked like

a regular mandarin. He had a golden pipe case in his hands
and he was gloating over it like a miser over his gold.

"There's Yuen Tang," I whispered.

"Yuen Tang my pet pig's knuckle," snorted Bill. "That's
Tung Yin hisself."

The Chinaman heard us and his head jerked up. His
eyes flared and then narrowed wickedly. He stuck the case
back in his blouse, quick but fumbling, like anybody does
when they're in a desperate hurry to keep somebody from
seeing something.

His other hand went inside his waist-sash and come
out with a snub-nosed pistol. But before he could use it,
me and Bill hit him simultaneous, one on the jaw and one
behind the ear. Either punch woulda settled his hash. The
both of 'em together dropped him like a pole-axed steer.
The gun flew outa his hand and he hit the floor so hard the
golden pipe case dropped outa his blouse and fell open on
the floor.

"Let's get going before he comes to," said I impatiently,
but Bill had stopped and was stooping with his hands on his
knees, eying the pipe case covetously.

"Boy, oh boy," he said. "Ain't that some outfit? I betcha
it cost three or four hundred bucks. I wisht I was rich. Them
Chinee merchant princes sure spread theirselves when it
comes to elegance."

23

I looked into the case which laid open on the floor. They was a small pipe with a slender amber stem and a ivory bowl, finely carved and yellow with age, some extra stems, a small silver box of them funny looking Chinese matches, and a golden rod for cleaning the pipe.

"By golly," said Bill, "I always wanted one of them ivory pipes."

"Hey," I said, "You can't hook Tung Yin's pipe. He ain't a-goin' to like it."

"Aw, it won't be stealin'," said Bill. "I'll leave him mine. 'Course it's made outa bone instead of ivory, but it cost me a dollar'n a half. Wonder you didn't bust it while ago when we was fightin'. I'll change pipes with him and he won't notice it till we're outa his reach."

"Well, hustle, then," I said impatiently. "I don't hold with no such graft, but what can you expect of a mutt from the Dutchman? Hurry up, before Tung Yin comes to and cuts our heads off."

So Bill took the ivory pipe and put his pipe in the case and shut the case up and stuck it back in Tung Yin's blouse. And we hustled. We come out into the courtyard. They wasn't no lanterns hanging there, or if they was they wasn't lighted, but the moon had come up and it was bright as day.

AND WE RAN RIGHT SMACK into Miss Kit Worley. There she was, dressed in flying togs and carrying a helmet in her hand. She gasped when she seen us.

"Good heavens," she said. "What are you doing here?"

"I come here to see you, Miss Worley," I said. "And Tung Yin made out like he was a servant tryin' to save me from his master, and gimme a gun and sent me into a dark room and, meanwhile, Bill had come buttin' in where he hadn't no business and they worked the same gag on him and we purty near kilt each other before we found out who we was."

She nodded, kind of bewildered, and then her eyes gleamed.

"I see," she said. "I see." She stood there twirling her helmet a minute, kind of studying, then she laid her hands on our shoulders and smiled very kindly and said: "Boys, I wish you'd do me a favor. I'm leaving in a few minutes by plane and I have a package that must be delivered. Will you boys deliver it?"

"Sure," we said. So she took out a small square package and said: "Take this to the Red Dragon. You know where that is? Sure you would. Well, go in and give it to the proprietor, Kang Woon. Don't give it to anyone else. And when you hand it to him, say, 'Tung Yin salutes you.' Got that straight?"

"Yeah," said Bill. "But gee whiz, Miss Worley, we can't leave you here to the mercy of them yellow-skinned cut-throats."

"Don't worry." She smiled. "I can handle Tung Yin. Go now, please. And thank you."

Well, she turned and went on in the house. We listened a minute and heard somebody howling and cussing in Chinese, and knowed Tung Yin had come to. We was fixing to go in and rescue Miss Worley, when we heard her talking to him, sharp and hard-like. He quieted down purty quick, so we looked at each other plumb mystified, and went on out in the garden and found the gate Bill come in at and went through it. We hadn't gone but a few yards when Bill says: "Dern it, Steve, I've lost that pipe I took offa Tung Yin."

"Well, gee whiz," I said disgustedly. "You ain't goin' back to look for it."

"I had it just before we come outa the garden," he insisted. So I went back with him, though highly disgusted, and he opened the gate and said: "Yeah, here it is. I musta dropped it as I started through the gate. Got a hole in my pocket."

About that time we seen three figgers in the moonlight crossing the garden--Miss Worley, Tung Yin and a slim, dark young fellow I knowed must be Clanry, the Australian aviator. All of 'em was dressed for flying, though Tung Yin looked like he'd just dragged on his togs recent. He looked kind of disrupted generally. As we looked we seen Miss Worley grab his arm and point and as Tung Yin turned his head, Clanry hit him from behind, hard, with a blackjack. For the second time that night the merchant prince took the count.

Miss Worley bent over him, tore his jacket open and jerked out that same golden pipe case. Then her and Clanry ran for a gate on the opposite side of the garden. They went through, leaving it open in their haste and then we saw 'em running through the moonlight to the plane, which lay amongst the orange groves. They reached it and right away we heard the roar of the propeller. They took off perfect and soared away towards the stars and outa sight.

As we watched, we heard the sound of fast driving autos. They pulled up in front of the place. We heard voices shouting commands in English and Chinese. Then Tung Yin stirred and staggered up, holding his head. From inside the house come the sound of doors being busted open and a general ruckus. Tung Yin felt groggily inside his blouse, then tore his hair, shook his fists at the sky, and run staggeringly across the garden to vanish through the other gate.

"What you reckon this is all about?" wondered Bill. "How come Miss Worley wanted Tung Yin's pipe, you reckon?"

"How should I know?" I replied. "Come on. This ain't any of our business. We got to deliver this package to Kang Woon."

So we faded away. And as we done so a backward look showed men in uniform ransacking the house and estate of Tung Yin.

No 'rickshas being available, we was purty tired when we come to the Red Dragon, in the early hours of morning. It was a low class dive on the waterfront which stayed open all night. Just then, unusual activity was going on. A bunch of natives was buzzing around the entrance and some Chinese police was shoving them back.

"Looks like Kang Woon's been raided," I grunted.

"That's it," said Bill. "Well, I been expectin' it, the dirty rat. I know he sells opium and I got a good suspicion he's a fence, too."

WE WENT UP TO THE DOOR and the Chinese cops wasn't going to let us in. We was about to haul off and sock 'em, when some autos drove up and stopped and a gang of soldiers with a Chinese officer and a English officer got out. They had a battered looking Chinaman with 'em in handcuffs. He was the one me and Bill socked and locked up in the murder room. They all went in and we fell in behind 'em and was in the dive before the cops knowed what we was doing.

It was a raid all right. The place was full of men in the uniform of the Federal army and the Chinese constabulary. Some of 'em--officers, I reckon--was questioning the drunks and beggars they'd found in the place. Over on one side was a cluster of Chinamen in irons, amongst them Kang Woon, looking like a big sullen spider. He was being questioned, but his little beady black eyes glinted dull with murder and he kept his mouth shut.

"There's the mutt which butted in, on our fight," grunted Bill in disgust.

One of the men questioning Kang Woon was Sir Peter Brent; the others was a high rank Chinese officer and a plain clothes official of some sort.

The British officer we'd followed in saluted and said: "I regret to report, Sir Peter, that the birds have flown the bally coop. We found the house deserted and showing signs of a recent and hurried evacuation. We found this Chinaman lying unconscious in an inner chamber which was locked from the outside, but we've gotten nothing out of him. We heard a plane just as we entered the house and I greatly fear that the criminals have escaped by air. Of Tung Yin and the others we found no trace at all, and though we made a careful search of the premises, we did not discover the gem."

"We did not spring the trap quick enough," said Sir Peter. "I should have suspected that they would be warned."

Well, while they was talking, me and Bill went up to Kang Woon and handed him the package. He shrunk back and glared like we was trying to hand him a snake, but we'd been told to give it to him, so we dropped it into his lap and said: "Tung Yin salutes you," just like Miss Worley had told us. The next minute we was grabbed by a horde of cops and soldiers.

"Hey," yelled Bill wrathfully. "What kinda game is this?" And he stood one of 'em on the back of his neck with a beautiful left hook.

I'm a man of few words and quick action. I hit one of 'em in the solar plexus and he curled up like a snake. We was fixing to wade through them deluded heathens like a whirlwind through a cornfield when Sir Peter sprang forward.

"Hold hard a bit, lads," he ordered. "Let those men go."

They fell away from us and me and Bill faced the whole gang belligerently, snorting fire and defiance.

"I know these men." he said. "They're honest American sailors."

"But they gave this to the prisoner," said the Chinese official, holding up the package.

"I know," said Sir Peter. "But if they're mixed up in this affair, I'm certain it's through ignorance rather than intent. They're rather dumb, you know."

Me and Bill was speechless with rage. The official said: "I'm not so sure."

THE OFFICIAL OPENED the package and said: "Ah, just as I suspected. The very case in which the gem was stolen."

He held it up and it was a jewel case with the arms of the old Chinese empire worked on it in gold. Kang Woon glowered at it and his eyes was Hell's fire itself.

"Now look." The official opened it and we all gasped. Inside was a large white gem which sparkled and glittered like ice on fire. The handcuffed Chinaman gave a howl and kind of collapsed.

"The Royal Crystal," cried the official in delight. "The stolen gem itself. Who gave you men this package?"

"None of your blamed business," I growled and Bill snarled agreement.

"Arrest them," exclaimed the official, but Sir Peter interposed again. "Wait." And he said to us: "Now, lads, I believe you're straight, but you'd best come clean, you know."

We didn't say nothing and he said: "Perhaps you don't know the facts of the case. This stone--which is of immense value--was stolen from the governmental museum. We know that it was stolen by a gang of international thieves who have been masquerading as honest merchants and traders. This gang consisted of Tung Yin, Clanry the aviator, a number of lesser crooks who pretended to be in Tung Yin's employ, and a girl called Clever Kit Worley."

"Hey, you," said Bill. "You lay offa Miss Worley."

"Aha," said Sir Peter, "I fancied I'd strike fire there. Now come, lads, didn't Clever Kit give you that stone?"

31

We still didn't say nothing. About that time the Chinaman the soldiers had brung with them hollered: "I'll tell. I'll tell it all. They've betrayed me and left me to go to prison alone, have they? Curse them all!"

He was kind of hysterical, but talked perfect English--was educated at Oxford, I learned later. Everybody looked at him and he spilled the beans so fast his words tripped over each other: "Tung Yin, Clanry and the Worley woman stole the Royal Crystal. They were equal partners in all the crimes they committed. We--the coolies, the dancing girls and I--were but servants, doing their bidding, getting no share of the loot, but being paid higher salaries than we could have earned honestly. Oh, it was a business proposition, I tell you.

"Tonight we got the tip that the place was to be raided--Tung Yin has plenty of spies. No sooner had we received this information than these sailors came blundering in, hunting Kit Worley, who had charmed them as she has so many men. The woman and Clanry were not in the house. They were preparing the plane for a hurried flight. Tung Yin supposed these men to be spies of the government, so he sent some of his servants to beguile the one, while he donned a disguise of menial garments and befooled the other. We sent them into a dark chamber to slay each other. And, meanwhile, we hurried our plans for escape.

"Clanry, the Worley woman and Tung Yin were planning to escape in the plane, and they promised to take me with them. Tung Yin told the coolies and dancing girls to save themselves as best they could. They scattered, looting the house as they fled. Then Tung Yin told me to look into the death chamber and see if the two foreign devils had killed each other. I did so--and was knocked senseless. What happened then I can only guess, but that Tung Yin, Clanry and Kit Worley escaped in the plane, I am certain, though how these men came to have the gem is more than I can say."

"I believe I can answer that," said Sir Peter. "I happen to know that Kang Woon here has been handling stolen goods for the Tung Yin gang. That's why we raided him tonight at the same time we sent a squad to nab the others at Tung Yin's place. But as you've seen, we were a bit too late. Kang Woon had advanced them quite a bit of money already for the privilege of handling the stone for them--the amount to be added to his commission when the gem was sold. The sale would have made them all rich, even though they found it necessary to cut it up and sell it in smaller pieces. They dared not skip without sending this stone to Kang Woon, for he knew too much. But watch."

He laid the gem on a table and hit it with his pistol butt and smashed it into bits. Everybody gawped. Kang Woon gnashed his teeth with fury.

"A fake, you see," said Sir Peter. "I doubt if any but an expert could have told the difference. I happen to have had quite a bit of experience in that line, don't you know. Yes, Tung Yin and Kit Worley and Clanry planned to double-cross Kang Woon. They sent him this fake, knowing that they would be out of his reach before he learned of the fraud. He's an expert crook, but not a jewel expert, you know. And now I suppose Tung Yin and his pals are safely out of our reach with the Royal Crystal."

WHILE WE WAS LISTENING Bill took out the pipe he'd stole from Tung Yin and began to cram tobaccer in it. He cussed disgustedly.

"Hey, Steve," said he. "What you think? Somebody's gone and crammed a big piece of glass into this pipe bowl." He was trying to work it loose.

"Gimme that pipe," I hollered and jerked it outa his hands. Disregarding his wrathful protests, I opened my knife and pried and gouged at the pipe bowl until the piece of glass rolled into my hand. I held it up and it caught the candle lights with a thousand gleams and glittering sparkles.

"The Royal Crystal," howled the Chinese. And Sir Peter grabbed it.

"By Jove," he exclaimed. "It's the real gem, right enough. Where did you get it?"

"Well," I said, "I'll tell you. Seein' as how Miss Worley is done got away and you can't catch her and put her in jail-

-and I don't mind tellin' you I'm glad of it, 'cause she mighta been a crook but she was nice to me. I see now why she and Clanry wanted that pipe case. It was a slick place to hide the gem in, but nothin's safe from one of them thieves offa the Dutchman. Tung Yin was goin' to double-cross Kang Woon and Clanry and Miss Worley double-crossed Tung Yin, but I betcha they look funny when they open that golden pipe case and find nothin' in it but Bill's old pipe."

"Aw," said Bill, "I betcha she keeps it to remember me by. I betcha she'll treasure it amongst her dearest soovernears."

Sir Peter kind of tore his hair and moaned: "Will you blighters tell us what it's all about and how you came by that gem?"

"Well," I said, "Tung Yin evidently had the gem in his pipe and Bill stole his pipe. And ... Well, it's a long story."

"Well, I'll be damned," said Sir Peter. "The keenest minds in the secret service fail and a pair of blundering bone-headed sailors succeed without knowing what it's all about."

"Well," said Bill impatiently, "if you mutts are through with me and Steve, we aims for to go forth and seek some excitement. Up to now this here's been about the tiresomest shore leave I've had yet."

THE END